THIS BOOK
BELONGS TO

_____

THE AIRY TALE TLAS

Written by
Courtney Acampora and Maggie Fischer

Silver Dolphin

CONTENTS

ONCE

UPON A TIME . . .

Alice's Adventures in Wonderland

Written in 1865, *Alice's Adventures in Wonderland* by Lewis Carroll is one of the most treasured children's stories. One afternoon, a young girl named Alice sits with her sister on a riverbank when she suddenly sees an unusual sight—a white rabbit in a waistcoat, frantically running by. Alice follows the rabbit down a rabbit hole, and into the mysterious world of Wonderland. In Wonderland, Alice encounters a cast of crazy characters including the Caterpillar, Cheshire Cat, Mad Hatter and March Hare, the Duchess, and the Queen of Hearts. Alice's journey through Wonderland takes her to the White Rabbit's house, a mad tea party, a game of croquet with the hotheaded Queen of Hearts, and much more. Around each corner, Alice experiences an event "curiouser and curiouser" than the last one. *Alice's Adventures in Wonderland* is full of whimsical and mad characters that bring Alice on an unforgettable journey.

Alice

Alice is a young girl with a vibrant imagination and curiosity for the world around her. In Wonderland, Alice is confronted with unusual experiences and nonsensical characters. Alice is a sensible and logical girl, so she finds herself constantly questioning the madness she runs into in Wonderland. Whether it's a little bottle with a message "drink me" or catching the Duchess's baby, who resembles a piglet, Alice experiences all sorts of strange things in Wonderland.

HAIR COLOR: Gold as the White Rabbit's pocket watch

EYE COLOR: Blue as a pool of tears

LIKES:
- Books with pictures, conversation
- Her cat, Dinah
- Lazy afternoons on a riverbank with her sister

DISLIKES:
- Riddles without answers
- Rudeness
- One confusing creature after another

White Rabbit

The White Rabbit is a busy bunny who dresses in a fine waistcoat and keeps time with his pocket watch. It is because of the White Rabbit that Alice enters Wonderland in the first place. The White Rabbit is an anxious creature whose biggest concern is being on time.

FUR COLOR: White as a rose

EYE COLOR: Pink as a flamingo mallet

LIKES:
- Sharp waistcoats
- Being on time
- Fans and white gloves

DISLIKES:
- Angering the Queen
- An overgrown Alice inside his home

Cheshire Cat

The Cheshire Cat is a mysterious, grinning creature. This cat knows all the workings of Wonderland and claims that Wonderland is mad, everyone who resides there is mad, and Alice herself is mad. The Cheshire Cat has the ability to vanish in thin air and partially reappear. During the game of croquet, the king quite dislikes the Cheshire Cat and calls for it to be beheaded . . . despite the fact that, at the time, only the Cheshire Cat's head is seen.

FUR COLOR: Purple as a dodo bird

EYE COLOR: Yellow as a slice of buttered bread

LIKES:
- Sitting in trees
- Vanishing and reappearing
- Grinning

DISLIKES:
- Giving directions
- The king, for ordering it to be beheaded

Queen of Hearts

The Queen of Hearts is the ruler of Wonderland and constantly announces that everyone should be beheaded. Everyone in Wonderland lives in fear of the Queen, except outspoken Alice . . . so the Queen of Hearts declares that Alice, too, should be beheaded.

EYE COLOR: Black as a spade

HAIR COLOR: Black as an inkstand

LIKES:
- Declaring "Off with their heads!"
- Red roses
- Croquet

DISLIKES:
- The Knave of Hearts
- White roses
- Alice talking back

"Soon her eye fell on a little glass box that was lying under the table: she opened it, and found in it a very small cake, on which the words 'Eat Me' were beautifully marked in currants. 'Well, I'll eat it,' said Alice, 'and if it makes me grow larger, I can reach the key; and if it makes me grow smaller, I can creep under the door . . .'"

Alice falls down the rabbit hole and lands in a hallway, where there is a small door she decides to go through. After drinking from a little bottle and shrinking down to only ten inches, Alice eats a cake with the hope that she'll grow larger. Instead, the little cake makes Alice grow more than nine feet tall. Alice becomes upset and begins to cry a pool of tears.

"The cat only grinned when it saw Alice. It looked goodnatured, she thought: still it had very long claws and a great many teeth, so she felt it ought to be treated with respect."

Alice sees the Cheshire Cat lounging in a tree and she asks it for directions. The Cheshire Cat is not very helpful, and it tells Alice that it doesn't matter which way she goes. The Cheshire Cat says that everyone in Wonderland is mad. Alice is not surprised when the Cheshire Cat vanishes and reappears because she becomes quite used to strange things happening in Wonderland.

"'The table was a large one, but the three were all crowded together at one corner of it: 'No room! No room!' they cried out when they saw Alice coming. 'There's plenty of room!' said Alice indignantly, and she sat down in a large arm-chair at the end of the table."

Alice joins the March Hare, the Mad Hatter, and the sleepy Dormouse for an eventful tea party. The moment Alice joins the tea party, she hears nonsensical riddles from the Mad Hatter and March Hare. At the table, it is always teatime and the Mad Hatter and March Hare move seats when they need new tea things. After the Dormouse tells a puzzling story, Alice can no longer take the madness, so she gets up and exclaims, "It's the stupidest tea party I ever was at in all my life."

"'Off with her head!' the Queen shouted at the top of her voice. Nobody moved.
'Who cares for you?' said Alice (she had grown to her full size by this time). 'You're nothing but a pack of cards!'
At this the whole pack rose up into the air, and came flying down upon her."

Inside the Court of Justice, the Knave of Hearts is being tried for stealing the Queen's tarts. The White Rabbit reads a poem as evidence. Alice declares that it is nonsense, which causes the Queen to become angry and to try to have Alice beheaded. The cards attack Alice, and when she bats them away, she wakes on the riverbank in her sister's lap, as leaves flutter down on her face.

Jack and the Beanstalk

"Jack and the Beanstalk" was adapted by Joseph Jacobs, an English writer, in 1890, but the basis for the story was written in 1734 by another writer. "Jack and the Beanstalk" follows a boy named Jack who lives with his widowed mother and their cow, named Milky-White. Jack and his mother are poor, and earn money from the milk that they sell. One day, Milky-White has no milk, so Jack must sell the cow. But instead of selling the cow, Jack is lured into trading Milky-White for a handful of magical beans. Jack plants the beans that night, and in the morning, awakes to a giant beanstalk that reaches the clouds.

Jack climbs the beanstalk and finds a house where a giant woman lives with her husband, an ogre. The ogre has an appetite for children, so Jack is forced to hide from him. Jack climbs up and down the beanstalk, stealing the ogre's treasures so that he can provide for his mother and himself. He steals gold and a hen that lays golden eggs, but when Jack tries to steal a golden harp, the harp shrieks and wakes the ogre. "Jack and the Beanstalk" is a story full of adventure and bravery as Jack faces a giant ogre.

Jack

Jack is a curious young boy who lives with his widowed mother. When his mother asks Jack to sell their cow in the village, he instead trades the cow for some magic beans that grow into a giant beanstalk. When Jack discovers a giant woman, an ogre, and all their riches at the top of the beanstalk, he seizes his opportunity to steal gold and other riches to make up for not selling Milky-White. Jack is brave, bold, and fast on his feet, all characteristics that help him when he is finally noticed by the ogre.

HAIR COLOR: Gold as the magic harp

EYE COLOR: Green as a beanstalk

LIKES:
- Gold and treasure
- Fooling giant ogres
- Magic beans

DISLIKES:
- Being chased by an ogre
- Going to bed without supper

12

Jack's Mother

A widow who supports her son Jack and herself by selling Milky-White's milk. When Milky-White doesn't have any milk one day, Jack's mother convinces him to sell the cow. She is surprised and angered when Jack returns with magic beans. Because of her son's bravery and risk-taking, she is able to live a rich and happy life.

HAIR COLOR: Gold as a bag of coins

EYE COLOR: Green as a handful of magic beans

LIKES:
- Gold and treasure
- Helping her son defeat the ogre

DISLIKES:
- Magic beans
- Jack returning from the village without money

The Ogre

The ogre lives at the top of the beanstalk with his wife. The ogre has a big appetite and his favorite meal is boys broiled on toast. The ogre has a strong sense of smell—especially for the blood of Englishmen. After meals, the ogre's wife gives him some of his gold coins to look at, and he falls asleep. While the ogre snores over his treasures, Jack is able to run off with the gold coins and a hen.

HAIR COLOR: Black as Milky-White's spots

EYE COLOR: Brown as an ox

LIKES:
- Gold and treasure
- Boys on broiled toast
- Naps after breakfast

DISLIKES:
- Being tricked by a boy
- Stolen riches

The Ogre's Wife

When Jack climbs to the top of the beanstalk, he first sees the ogre's wife outside the home. Unlike her husband, the woman is friendly and feeds Jack instead of eating him. She warns Jack of her husband's appetite and helps Jack hide from the ogre.

HAIR COLOR: Brown as a loaf of bread

EYE COLOR: Blue as a pail of water

LIKES:
- Gathering her husband's riches
- Helping Jack hide from the ogre

DISLIKES:
- Lying to her husband
- Being called "Mum" by Jack

"'Ah! You don't know what these beans are,' said the man; 'if you plant them overnight, by morning they grow right up to the sky.'"

On the way to the village market, a man offers to buy Milky-White in exchange for some magic beans. After hearing about the beans' magic ability of growing up to the sky, Jack trades Milky-White. When Jack returns home, his mother is not pleased about the beans, so she tosses them out of the window.

"Jack jumped up and dressed himself and went to the window. And what do you think he saw? Why, the beans his mother had thrown out of the window into the garden had sprung up into a big beanstalk which went up and up and up till it reached the sky. So the man spoke truth after all."

When Jack wakes up in the morning, his room is shaded by the giant beanstalk growing right outside his window. Jack jumps out of his bedroom window and climbs the beanstalk all the way to the top.

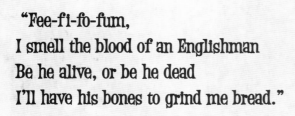

"Fee-fi-fo-fum,
I smell the blood of an Englishman
Be he alive, or be he dead
I'll have his bones to grind me bread."

The ogre has a strong sense of smell, and he tromps into the kitchen exclaiming that he smells a boy. The old woman protects Jack by saying that the ogre must be smelling the scraps of the boy he ate yesterday. This response satisfies the ogre, and he washes up for breakfast, eats, then counts his bag of gold. It's not until Jack's third trip up the beanstalk that the ogre actually sees Jack—with the help of the golden harp's shrieking.

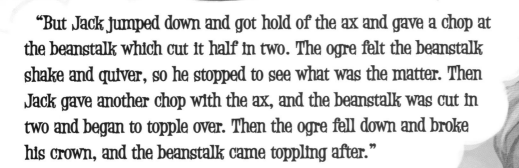

"But Jack jumped down and got hold of the ax and gave a chop at the beanstalk which cut it half in two. The ogre felt the beanstalk shake and quiver, so he stopped to see what was the matter. Then Jack gave another chop with the ax, and the beanstalk was cut in two and began to topple over. Then the ogre fell down and broke his crown, and the beanstalk came toppling after."

Jack tries to steal the golden harp but it shrieks "Master, Master!" and the ogre awakes and chases Jack. The ogre reaches the end of the road at the top of the beanstalk and swings down after Jack. Jack reaches the bottom of the beanstalk and asks his mother to bring him an axe. Once the beanstalk is cut, and the ogre is gone, Jack and his mother are able to live a life full of the ogre's riches.

The Ogre

Jack

The Little Mermaid

"The Little Mermaid" was written in 1837 by Hans Christian Andersen, a Danish author who wrote many fairy tales. In "The Little Mermaid," a young mermaid lives under the sea with her five sisters, her grandmother, and her father, the sea king. When the daughters each turn fifteen years old, they're allowed to swim to the ocean surface to see the world of humans. The little mermaid wants to see life above water most of all. On her fifteenth birthday, she swims to the surface and sees a handsome prince, whom she saves during a storm. The little mermaid wants nothing more than to fall in love with the prince and to gain a soul that lives on forever, something that mermaids don't have. With the help of a sea witch, the little mermaid trades her beautiful voice for human legs. However, the little mermaid is unable to turn back into a mermaid, and if the prince doesn't fall in love and marry her, she will die and turn to seafoam. Through the deep-sea kingdom to the ocean waves, the little mermaid risks her life for the chance at love.

The Little Mermaid

The little mermaid is the youngest daughter of the sea king who lives with her five older sisters and her grandmother. She is the most beautiful mermaid with soft skin and eyes as blue as the sea. She entertains herself with her undersea garden plot where she plants red flowers and has a marble statue shaped like a prince. The little mermaid is a quiet girl who loves to learn about the world of human beings.

HAIR COLOR: Gold as sun rays

EYE COLOR: Blue as the loveliest cornflower

LIKES:
- Seeing the human world
- The handsome prince
- Spending time in her garden

DISLIKES:
- Wearing a wreath of white lilies in her hair
- Leaving her family
- Not having a soul that lives on forever

Grandmother

The grandmother is the sea king's mother and is very fond of her six granddaughters. The grandmother tells her granddaughters stories about life above water. She also tells the little mermaid that humans do not live three hundred years like mermaids, humans instead have a soul that lives on forever.

HAIR COLOR: White as a glistening pearl

EYE COLOR: Blue as a crashing wave

LIKES:
- Flaunting twelve oysters on her tail
- Her granddaughters
- Telling stories about the world of humans

DISLIKES:
- Life without the little mermaid
- Losing her hair in grief

Sea Witch

The sea witch lives deep down in the sea, through whirlpools, in a forest made of polyps that are half snake and half plant. The sea witch lives in a house built from the bones of shipwrecked men. She is surrounded by her fat sea snakes, called chickabiddies. Knowing what the little mermaid wants, the sea witch makes a potion in her cauldron that turns the little mermaid's fin into human legs in exchange for her voice.

HAIR COLOR: Gray as a storm cloud

EYE COLOR: Yellow as an eel's underbelly

LIKES:
- Collecting the bones of shipwrecked men
- Mixing potions
- Gaining a beautiful singing voice

DISLIKES:
- Pricking herself to gather black blood for her potions
- Deciding which chickabiddie is her favorite

Prince

The prince is celebrating his birthday aboard a ship when he is suddenly thrown overboard and is saved by the little mermaid. Once the little mermaid's tail has transformed into legs, the prince sees the little mermaid and believes she looks similar to the girl who saved his life. The prince loves the little mermaid dearly, but he marries a human princess instead.

HAIR COLOR: Brown as a ship's wooden stern

EYE COLOR: Dark as the night sky

LIKES:
- The beautiful princess he marries
- Spending time with the little mermaid

DISLIKES:
- Storms and shipwrecks
- Not remembering who saved him from drowning

"She dived through the waves and rode their crests, until at length she reached the young prince, who was no longer able to swim in that raging sea. His arms and legs were exhausted, his beautiful eyes were closing, and he would have died if the little mermaid had not come to help him."

The little mermaid watches the handsome prince on the ship when suddenly a terrible storm occurs. The ship splits into two, and she sees the prince sink down in the sea. The little mermaid saves the prince by carrying him ashore, then she swims away before the prince realizes who saved him.

"'Also, you will have to pay me,' said the witch, 'and it is no trifling price that I'm asking. You have the sweetest voice of anyone down here at the bottom of the sea, and while I don't doubt that you would like to captivate the prince with it, you must give this voice to me.'"

Desperate to be reunited with the prince, the little mermaid visits the sea witch with the hope that she can transform her tail into human legs. In order to gain an immortal soul such as a human has, the prince must fall in love and marry the little mermaid. The sea witch mixes together a potion in her cauldron in exchange for the little mermaid's voice.

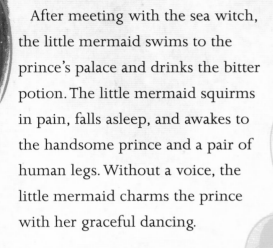

"When the sun rose over the sea, she awoke and felt a flash of pain, but directly in front of her stood the handsome young prince, gazing at her with his coal-black eyes. Lowering her gaze, she saw that her fish tail was gone and that she had the loveliest pair of white legs any young maid could hope to have."

After meeting with the sea witch, the little mermaid swims to the prince's palace and drinks the bitter potion. The little mermaid squirms in pain, falls asleep, and awakes to the handsome prince and a pair of human legs. Without a voice, the little mermaid charms the prince with her graceful dancing.

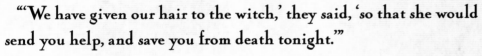

"'We have given our hair to the witch,' they said, 'so that she would send you help, and save you from death tonight.'"

On the night of the prince's wedding, the little mermaid's sisters tell her that in exchange for their hair, the witch gave them a knife so the little mermaid could kill the prince. If she struck the prince's heart, the little mermaid's tail would grow back, and she could return to the sea. But the little mermaid refuses to hurt the prince, choosing instead to turn into seafoam. Because of her good deed, the little mermaid is turned into a daughter of air, a spirit given the chance to gain a soul that lives on forever. As a daughter of air, the little mermaid has three hundred years to gain a soul that lives on forever.

Palace of the
Sea King

Mermaids'
Garden

Sea
Witch's
Home

Forest
of Polyps

Prince's
Palace

Hansel and Gretel

The classic tale of "Hansel and Gretel" was written by the Brothers Grimm in 1812. The Brothers Grimm were German brothers who wrote a collection of fairy tales. In "Hansel and Gretel," Hansel and his sister, Gretel, live at the edge of the forest with their father, a woodcutter, and their stepmother, who is not very fond of the children. Their evil stepmother convinces their father that the family is too poor, and they cannot afford to feed the children. She forms a plan to tell the children they are all going to fetch firewood in the woods, where the parents would leave them, far from home. The stepmother tries to abandon the children, but Hansel is a clever boy who leaves a trail of pebbles back to his home. When the children are again taken to the woods, Hansel leaves a trail of breadcrumbs, which is, however eaten by birds, and the brother and sister become lost. Hansel and Gretel stumble upon a delicious home in the forest made from cakes and sweets. However, an evil witch lives inside and locks up Hansel so she can eat him.

Hansel and Gretel fool the witch, and ultimately Gretel pushes the witch into the oven. "Hansel and Gretel" is a story about children's bravery, perseverance, and their defeat of an evil witch.

Hansel

Gretel's older brother and the woodcutter's son, Hansel is a clever boy who doesn't trust his stepmother. Each time she leads the children deep into the forest, he leaves some kind of trail to mark the way back home. When the wicked witch forces Hansel to show her his finger each day to check that he is fattening up, Hansel fools the nearly blind witch by handing her a skinny chicken bone instead, giving him more time to come up with an escape plan.

HAIR COLOR: Yellow as a gum drop

EYE COLOR: Green as a witch's potion

LIKES:
- Outsmarting his stepmother
- Nibbling on the witch's roof
- Pretty little beds covered in clean white linen

DISLIKES:
- Having his breadcrumb trail eaten by birds
- Being locked up in a stable

Gretel

Hansel's younger sister, Gretel, is smart like her brother. She convinces the witch to look inside the oven, so she can shove the witch inside and escape with Hansel.

HAIR COLOR: Yellow as the witch's gold

EYE COLOR: Blue as a sparkling pond

LIKES:
- Shoving the witch in the oven
- Being reunited with Hansel

DISLIKES:
- Doing chores
- Eating crab shells

The Woodcutter

The woodcutter lives on the edge of a forest with his wife and two children, Hansel and Gretel. The woodcutter experiences hardships, which make it nearly impossible to feed his family.

HAIR COLOR: Gray as a storm cloud

EYE COLOR: Brown as chopped firewood

LIKES:
- Being reunited with his children
- Jewels and pearls brought home by Hansel and Gretel

DISLIKES:
- Abandoning Hansel and Gretel in the forest
- Not being able to feed his family

The Witch

The witch lives deep in the forest in a house made of sugar-paned windows with roofs and walls made of cakes and bread. The house lures Hansel and Gretel to the witch, whose favorite meal is lost children. The witch's end comes when she is pushed into the oven and burned.

HAIR COLOR: White as a pebble trail

EYE COLOR: Red as hot coals

LIKES:
- Eating children
- Building a house made of sweets to entice children

DISLIKES:
- Children not fattening up properly
- Blurry vision

25

"The father said, 'Now children, pile up some wood, and I will light a fire that you may not be cold.' Hansel and Gretel gathered brushwood together, as high as a little hill."

To bring the children to the middle of the forest, the woodcutter and his wife convince Hansel and Gretel that they are fetching wood. The children sit by the fire, waiting for their father and stepmother to finish chopping wood. Hansel and Gretel doze by the fire and later realize that their father and stepmother have deserted them in the forest.

"'Nibble, nibble, gnaw,
Who is nibbling at my little house?'
The children answered,
'The wind, the wind,
the heaven-born wind,'
and went on eating without
disturbing themselves."

When Hansel and Gretel awake in the woods, they spot a snow-white bird that leads the children to the witch's house. Located deep in the woods, the house is made of sweets and entices the children. After nibbling on the roof and windowpane, the children are welcomed inside the home. The witch prepares a big meal and offers the children two cozy beds. Hansel and Gretel then learn the witch's motive and her hunger for children. Next to the witch's house stands the stable where Hansel is locked up.

"Little duck, little duck, do you see,
Hansel and Gretel are waiting for you?
There's never a plank, or bridge in sight,
Take us across on your back so white."

After the witch is burned in the oven,
Hansel and Gretel fill their pockets with
the witch's jewels. Hansel and Gretel
trek through the forest, searching for a
familiar path home. Instead, the siblings
find a large body of water without a clear
passage across. Gretel spots a graceful
white duck, and she expertly uses her
duck-calling skills to give both her and
her brother rides across the lake.

"Then they began to run, rushed into the parlor, and threw themselves into their father's arms.
The man had not known one happy hour since he had left the children in the forest . . ."

Carrying the jewels and treasure they
took from the witch, Hansel and Gretel
are reunited with their father. They realize
their stepmother is gone, and their lives
are changed from rags to riches.

Hansel & Gretel

The Woods

Lake

Woodcutter's Home

Hansel's Pebble Trail

Witch's Home

Stable

Fire

Little Snow White

Written in 1812 by the Brothers Grimm, the story "Little Snow White" follows a beautiful girl named Snow White as she tries to escape from her wicked and jealous stepmother who is a queen. Snow White's stepmother has a special mirror, and when she asks the question "Who in this land is the fairest of all?" the looking glass will answer that the stepmother is the fairest. But much to the stepmother's dismay, one day the looking glass declares that Snow White is the most beautiful. This fills the stepmother with anger and rage, so she sends a hunter to kill Snow White and bring back her heart as proof. The hunter cannot bear to kill Snow White, so he tells the young girl to run away.

Snow White stumbles upon a cottage in the woods and meets seven dwarves who invite her to stay. The stepmother finds out that Snow White is alive, so she disguises herself as an old woman and tries to kill Snow White first with lace, then a poisoned comb, and finally a poisoned apple. After taking a bite of the apple, Snow White appears dead and is placed in a glass coffin by the dwarves. It's not until a handsome prince finds Snow White that the apple is removed from Snow White's throat, and she is brought back to life.

Snow White

The king's daughter and the subject of her stepmother's jealousy, Snow White is so beautiful that her stepmother's looking glass declares her as the fairest in the land. After she flees from the hunter, her stepmother hired to kill her, Snow White survives her stepmother's attempts on her life until she eats the poisoned apple, and she seemingly falls dead. A prince and his servants save the sleeping Snow White. Later, Snow White marries the prince and becomes a queen.

EYE COLOR: Black as a starry night

HAIR COLOR: Blue as a sapphire

LIKES:
- The seven dwarves' cottage
- The dwarves who take her in
- Princes who wander in the forest

DISLIKES:
- Her jealous stepmother
- Poisoned apples

Stepmother

After the king's first wife passes away, he marries a very vain woman who asks her magical looking glass to tell her that she is the most beautiful person in the land. When her stepdaughter grows up and surpasses her beauty, the stepmother does all she can to get rid of Snow White. The stepmother meets her end at Snow White's wedding when the prince forces the stepmother to wear hot iron slippers.

HAIR COLOR: Black as a hunter's arrow   **EYE COLOR:** Green with envy

LIKES:
- Using witchcraft to make a poisonous comb and apple
- Her looking glass (as long as it tells her she is the fairest of them all)

DISLIKES:
- Snow White's beauty
- Incompetent hunters

The Seven Dwarves

Deep inside the forest, the seven dwarves live in a little cottage that is "neater and cleaner than you can imagine." The dwarves let Snow White stay with them after she tells the dwarves about her stepmother and the hunter. Each day, the dwarves go into the mountains to mine copper and gold. After visits from the stepmother, the dwarves save Snow White. After she eats the poisoned apple, the dwarves grieve Snow White's death and make her a glass coffin so she can be seen from every angle.

HAIR COLOR: White as freshly fallen snow   **EYE COLOR:** Blue as a singing bird

LIKES:
- A house that is spic and span
- Mining for copper and gold

DISLIKES:
- Losing their sweet Snow White
- Snow White not listening to their advice

Prince

When the king's son is in the woods, he sees the glass coffin with Snow White inside. Snow White is so beautiful that the prince wants to keep her. He begs the dwarves for the coffin at any price, and when they refuse, he asks if he can have it as a gift. After the dwarves give the prince Snow White's coffin, his servants trip on a tree stump, and the poisoned apple is jolted from Snow White's throat. Snow White is saved and falls in love with the king's son.

HAIR COLOR: Brown as a tree stump   **EYE COLOR:** Blue as an afternoon sky

LIKES:
- Stumbling upon a beautiful girl in a forest
- Saving the life of Snow White

DISLIKES:
- Snow White's envious stepmother
- Snow White's stepmother attending his wedding

"'Looking glass, Looking glass, on the wall,
Who in this land is the fairest of all?'
It answered—
'You are fairer than all who are here,
Lady Queen.
But more beautiful still is Snow White,
as I ween.'"

When Snow White's stepmother asks her magical looking glass who is the fairest in the land, and the response is Snow White, the stepmother turns green with envy and becomes determined to kill Snow White. After the stepmother attempts to kill Snow White, the looking glass tells the stepmother that Snow White is still alive.

"When it was morning, little Snow White awoke, and was frightened when she saw the seven dwarfs. But they were friendly and asked her what her name was. 'My name is Snow White,' she answered."

The dwarves' little cottage in the woods is the perfect refuge for Snow White. After hearing about her evil stepmother and the hunter who almost killed her, the dwarves let Snow White stay in their home as long as she helps them cook and clean. Before working in the mines, the dwarves warn Snow White to not let anyone in the cottage. After each of the stepmother's visits, it is the dwarves who find Snow White and save her.

"When she heard the glass speak, she trembled and shook with rage. 'Snow White shall die,' she cried, 'even if it costs me my life!'

With that, she went into a quite secret, lonely room, where no one ever came, and there she made a very poisonous apple."

Determined to once again be the fairest in the land, the stepmother takes it upon herself to poison an apple and get Snow White to eat it. The stepmother, disguised as an old woman, convinces Snow White to eat the poisoned skin as she eats the apple's inside. At last, it seems like the stepmother's plan has finally worked.

"'Oh, heavens, where am I?' she cried.

The king's son, full of joy, said, 'You are with me,' and told her what happened, and said, 'I love you more than everything in the world; come with me to my father's palace, you shall be my wife.'"

The piece of poisoned apple falls out of Snow White's throat, and when she opens her eyes, she sees the king's son. Snow White and the king's son have a splendid wedding at his palace. The stepmother is also invited to the wedding, though she is full of rage that Snow White, now a queen, is alive and still more beautiful than she.

Little Snow White

King's Castle

MINE

Evil Stepmother & Magic Mirror

Secret Lab

Snow White

THE FOREST

Peter Pan

Written in 1904 by J. M. Barrie, *Peter Pan* follows a boy who never grows up and his adventures in Neverland with children Wendy, John, and Michael. One evening at the Darling residence, a young girl named Wendy awakes in her nursery to find Peter Pan crying because he lost his shadow. Peter Pan teaches Wendy, John, and Michael how to fly and leads them to the magical island of Neverland. In Neverland, the Darling children visit a mermaid lagoon, meet the Lost Boys, and are captured by the infamous Captain Hook. After many adventures in Neverland, the Darling children return home. Wendy promises to go back to Neverland yearly for spring cleaning, but as Wendy grows up, Peter Pan and Neverland become a distant memory. Peter Pan, the boy who never grows up, visits Wendy's daughter, and the adventures of Neverland continue generation after generation.

Peter Pan

Peter Pan is an adventurous boy who never grows up and lives on a magical island called Neverland. Peter Pan visits the Darling children through their bedroom window, and invites them to fly to Neverland with him. Peter Pan is a clever boy who outsmarts and defeats Captain Hook, the most fearful pirate on the island.

HAIR COLOR: Brown as Slightly's tree trunk

EYE COLOR: Green as a mermaid's tail

LIKES:
- Bedtime stories
- Outsmarting Captain Hook
- Mimicking the sounds of a ticking crocodile

DISLIKES:
- Losing his shadow
- Growing up
- Laziness

Wendy

Wendy is the oldest of the Darling children, and she is the one who sees Peter in the nursery and helps him reattach his missing shadow. Wendy is a caring girl who takes on a motherly role with her siblings, Peter, and the Lost Boys. Wendy loves adventure, and in adulthood she becomes a loving mother to her own daughter.

HAIR COLOR: Brown as the bow of the *Jolly Roger*

EYE COLOR: Blue as a sparkling waterfall

LIKES:

- Telling the Lost Boys stories
- Pretending to be a mother
- Mermaids

DISLIKES:

- Being attacked by Tinker Bell
- Being shot by Tootle's arrow

Captain Hook

Captain Hook is the leader of the pirates in Neverland. He dislikes Peter most of all because he thinks Peter is overly confident. During a duel, Peter cut off Captain Hook's hand and flung it into the water. A hungry crocodile ate Hook's hand, and whenever he sees or hears the crocodile, Captain Hook runs away in fear. Captain Hook's missing hand was replaced with an iron hook. Peter Pan and Captain Hook have a final battle that ends with Hook being eaten by the feared crocodile.

HAIR COLOR: Black as Marooners' Rock

EYE COLOR: Black as a pirate flag

LIKES:

- Being the most feared pirate in Neverland
- Bossing around his right-hand man Smee

DISLIKES:

- The crocodile
- Only having one hand
- Anything Peter Pan does

Tinker Bell

Tinker Bell is a fairy that accompanies Peter Pan. She joins Peter when he visits the Darling children's nursery, and she is very jealous of Peter's relationship with Wendy. When she's upset, Tinker Bell uses foul language and aggressive behavior. Tinker Bell is very loyal to Peter and almost dies in order to save his life.

HAIR COLOR: Gold as fairy dust

EYE COLOR: Green as a crocodile's back

LIKES:

- Being loyal and sticking by Peter Pan
- Children who believe in fairies
- Mending pots and kettles

DISLIKES:

- Peter Pan giving other girls attention
- Being shut inside drawers
- Helping Wendy

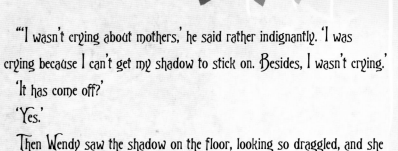

"'I wasn't crying about mothers,' he said rather indignantly. 'I was crying because I can't get my shadow to stick on. Besides, I wasn't crying.'
'It has come off?'
'Yes.'
Then Wendy saw the shadow on the floor, looking so draggled, and she was frightfully sorry for Peter."

Peter Pan and Tinker Bell enter the Darling nursery searching for Peter's missing shadow. When his shadow doesn't stick with a bar of soap, Peter sobs with frustration. Peter's crying wakes Wendy, who is introduced to Peter. Wendy sews Peter's shadow back on. Peter tells Wendy that he has been listening to Mrs. Darling's bedtime stories because he and the Lost Boys don't know any stories. Peter invites Wendy to Neverland to tell stories to the Lost Boys.

"'Where am I?' she said.
Of course Slightly was the first to get his word in. 'Wendy lady,' he said rapidly, 'for you we built this house.'
'Oh, say you're pleased,' cried Nibs.
'Lovely, darling house,' Wendy said, and they were the very words they had hoped she would say.
'And we are your children,' cried the twins.
Then all went on their knees, and holding out their arms cried, 'O Wendy lady, be our mother.'"

Tootles mistakes the flying Wendy for a bird and shoots her with an arrow. When she falls to the ground, the Lost Boys are saddened to realize that they've hurt a lady. Peter Pan explains to the boys that he has brought them a mother to tell them stories and is angry with the Lost Boys and Tinker Bell, who convinced Tootles to shoot Wendy. As Wendy awakens, the Lost Boys build a house around her and she takes on the role of a loving mother to the Lost Boys.

"'Why Tink, how dare you drink my medicine?'
But she did not answer. Already she was reeling in the air.
'What is the matter with you?' cried Peter, suddenly afraid.
'It was poisoned, Peter,' she told him softly; 'and now I am going to be dead.'
'O Tink, did you drink it to save me?'"

After the Lost Boys, Wendy, John, and Michael are captured by the pirates, Captain Hook secretly poisons Peter Pan's medicine while he sleeps. Tinker Bell tries to warn Peter about the poisoned medicine, but he doesn't believe her. Tinker Bell drinks the medicine to save Peter. Luckily, fairies can be saved when children around the world believe in fairies and clap their hands. Children everywhere begin clapping, which saves Tinker Bell's life.

"Seeing Peter slowly advancing upon him through the air with dagger poised, he sprang upon the Bulwarks to cast himself into the sea. He did not know that the crocodile was waiting for him; for we purposely stopped the clock that this knowledge might be spared him."

Peter Pan sneaks onto the pirate ship where the children are chained up. Cleverly disguised as Wendy, he frees everyone. When Peter is revealed, Hook is caught off guard, and the final battle begins. Captain Hook's fear of the crocodile becomes a reality when Peter Pan and Hook fight, and Captain Hook falls into the sea and into the crocodile's mouth.

PETER PAN
INDIAN CAMP
MAROONERS' ROCK
NEVERLAND
CROCODILE CREEK
LONDON
DARLINGS' HOUSE

THE DARLING CHILDREN

Peter
Pan

SKULL ROCK

THE JOLLY ROGER

Mermaid
Lagoon

CANNIBAL
COVE

Lost Boys

Aladdin and the Wonderful Lamp

"Aladdin and the Wonderful Lamp" was written as a part of *Arabian Nights*, a collection of Middle Eastern folktales by an unknown number of authors. Life changes for down-on-his-luck Aladdin when he meets a charming man claiming to be his uncle. A magician from Morroco, the man gives Aladdin a shop of his own to make his living and shows him all the wonders of the city. One evening, the two men happen upon a narrow valley. The Moroccan magician reveals a trapdoor in the valley and encourages Aladdin to go inside and fetch him an old lamp. Aladdin obeys, taking the magician's ring as a show of support. Once he finds the lamp, Aladdin refuses to hand it over until he is entirely out of the trapdoor, enraging the man and making him slam the door on Aladdin. Hearing a stone being pushed in front of the door, Aladdin realizes that the man was not his uncle and that he is well and truly trapped. With no way out, Aladdin discovers both the ring and the lamp are magical—each contains a genie willing to do his bidding. Through the magic of the lamp, he grows rich beyond his wildest dreams, marries the Sultan's daughter, and builds a palace more magnificent than has ever been seen. But good fortune comes with a price, and the Moroccan magician seeks revenge for losing the lamp. Aladdin's journey becomes dangerous, and he must find a way to take care of what he has before it gets taken away!

Aladdin

Lazy, but clever, Aladdin's dreams don't involve hard work. However, when the lamp falls into his hands, he is eager to gain the life he feels he deserves. He falls for the beautiful princess at first sight and tirelessly tries to impress her and earn her favor.

HAIR COLOR: Black as the inside of a deep cave

EYE COLOR: Black as a scarab beetle

LIKES:
- Winning the hand of Lady Badr al-Budur
- Convenient magic lamps
- Making wishes

DISLIKES:
- The Moroccan magician and his brother
- Hard work
- Dark caves

Moroccan Magician

Manipulative, cunning, and ruthless, the Moroccan magician has no problem lying or stealing to get what he wants. His intelligence and determination to gain wealth and power at any cost make him a dangerous man to know.

HAIR COLOR: Black as sinister magic

EYE COLOR: Black as a sunless sky

LIKES:	DISLIKES:
- Power	- Aladdin
- Riches	- Lack of control
- Magic	- Poison

Lady Badr al-Budur

Reserved and easily frightened, the princess, Lady Lady Badr al-Budur finds herself in the middle of a battle of magic and power involving the Moroccan magician and Aladdin, and she is missing key parts of the story behind it. However, she loves Aladdin and is loyal to her family and her husband, trusting that they will ensure her happiness.

HAIR COLOR: Black as a raven's wing

EYE COLOR: Dark as molten amber

LIKES:	DISLIKES:
- Aladdin	- The Moroccan magician
- Her palace	- Being kidnapped
- Her handmaiden	- The Moroccan magician's brother

Moroccan Magician's Brother

Furious over the death of his brother at the hands of Aladdin, the Moroccan magician's younger brother seeks revenge and the magic lamp, as he, too, craves its power. Merciless and cruel, he is worse than the brother that came before him and even more determined, with vengeance on his mind.

HAIR COLOR: Black as midnight

EYE COLOR: Gold as a magic lamp

LIKES:	DISLIKES:
- Power	- Aladdin
- Riches	- Lady Badr al-Budur
- Magic	- Loose ends

"But when the Moorman saw that he would not hand it over, he waxed wroth with wrath exceeding and cut of all his hopes of winning it; so he conjured and adjured and cast incense amiddlemost the fire . . . and Aladdin, unable to issue forth, remained underground."

Left alone in the dark cave, Aladdin realizes that he has been trapped by the magician, who is not his uncle at all, but a power-hungry trickster. Desperate, he rubs the magician's ring and is greeted by a genie who helps him escape. Once home, he and his poor mother attempt to sell the lamp for money to buy food. When cleaning the lamp to sell, Aladdin's mother releases the genie in the lamp, and Aladdin's life is forever changed.

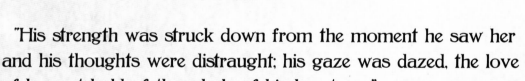

"His strength was struck down from the moment he saw her and his thoughts were distraught; his gaze was dazed, the love of her get hold of the whole of his heart . . ."

In love with the princess from the first look, Aladdin gives her father mountains of jewels to win her hand. The sultan's vizier convinces the ruler to wait three months before agreeing to Aladdin's proposal, giving other suitors a chance. In that time, the vizier's son nearly marries the princess, but Aladdin was determined to keep the sultan at his word as he loved the princess with all of his heart.

" . . . the Magician, having considered and ascertained that Aladdin had escaped from the souterrain and had gotten the boon of the Lamp, said to himself, 'There is no help but that I work for his destruction.'"

The magician returns to defeat Aladdin, and while Aladdin is away, the magician trades the princess a shiny new lamp for the one he knew to be magic. The wicked magician transports Aladdin's palace, wealth, and wife with him to Africa, leaving Aladdin with nothing.

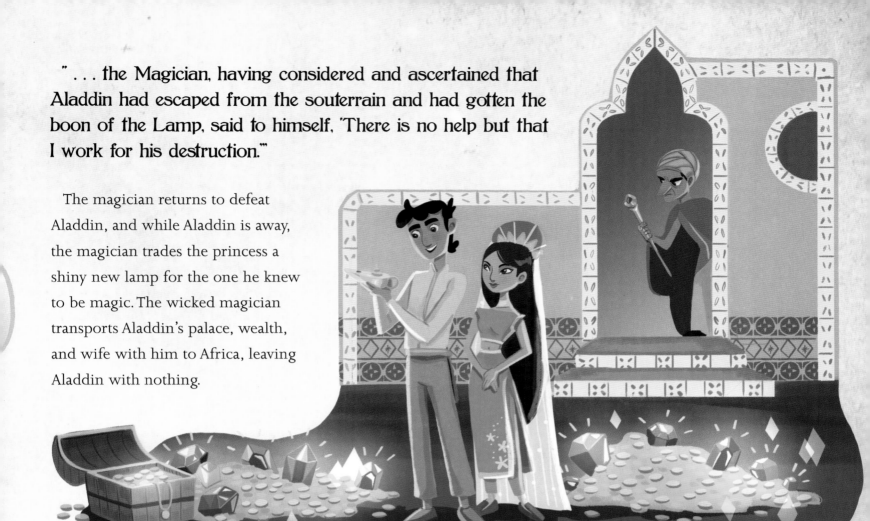

"When the Sultan drew near the latticed casement of his palace and looked over at Aladdin's pavilion he saw naught; nay, the site was smooth as a well-trodden highway . . ."

When the sultan discovers his daughter is missing, he is furious with Aladdin and the enchantments taking place around him. Aladdin convinces the sultan that he will find the princess. For weeks, Aladdin searches for his lost princess, finally finding her in the clutches of the magician. He rescues his wife and returns home with her, victorious, only to face the vengeance of the magician's younger brother. With the help of the genie, Aladdin defeats him, too.

Aladdin and the Wonderful Lamp

The Secret Cave

The Narrow Valley

Gardens

Aladdin's Palace

Aladdin's Palace
The Magician's Palace

The Wonderful Wizard of Oz

Written in 1900 by L. Frank Baum, *The Wonderful Wizard of Oz* is a tale of friendship, magic, and strength within one's heart. When a tornado touches down in Kansas, Dorothy Gale, her dog, Toto, and her aunt and uncle's farmhouse are all carried off into the sky. The house lands in a strange place known as The Land of the East, whose pint-sized citizens call themselves Munchkins. The Munchkins thank Dorothy, for her house landed on and vanquished the Wicked Witch of the East. In the Land of the East, Dorothy meets the Good Witch of the North, who advises her to go to the Emerald City and seek the Great and Terrible Wizard called Oz. The witch assures Dorothy that only the wizard will know how she can return home. On her journey across this magical land, she encounters three friends searching for things only the wizard can help them with: a scarecrow who desperately wants a brain, a tin woodman who needs a heart, and a cowardly lion who needs to find courage. But Dorothy and her friends must earn the things they want most by outsmarting the Wicked Witch of the West. Fighting against beasts, forces of nature, and the witch's magic, Dorothy and her friends travel through Oz and learn that everything is not always what it seems. But with courage, kindness, and the help of some sparkling silver shoes, Dorothy happily returns home.

Dorothy

A sweet, young girl, Dorothy simply wants to return home to Kansas to see her aunt and uncle. Brave enough to travel through foreign, frightening places to make her wish come true, she has a big heart that opens wide to welcome new friends and her dear dog, Toto.

HAIR COLOR: Brown as the earth on her aunt and uncle's farm

EYE COLOR: Brown as dry Kansas grass

LIKES:
- Her home, Kansas
- Her dog, Toto
- The Good Witches of the North and South

DISLIKES:
- The Wicked Witch of the West
- The scarlet poppies
- Being far from home

The Scarecrow

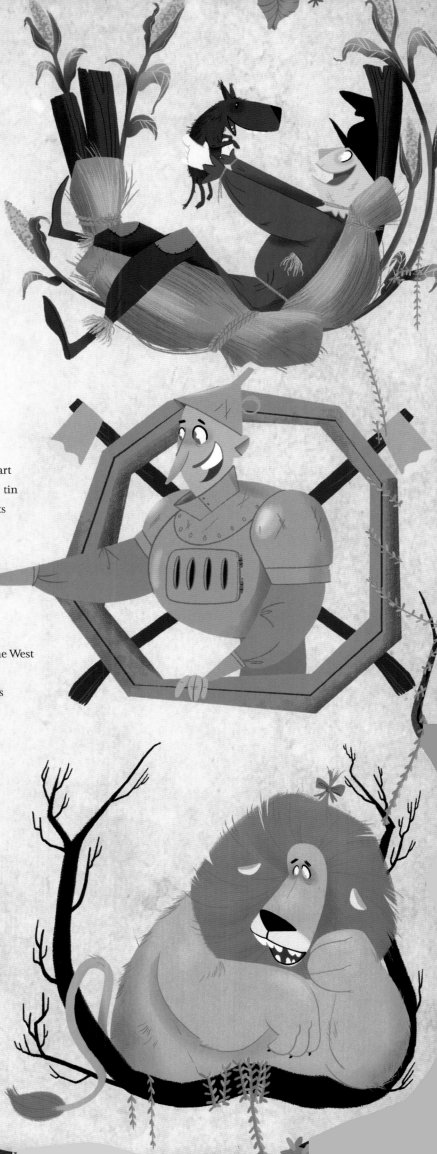

The scarecrow wants to do more than simply frighten crows away from crops. And in order to be more than just a prop in the field, he wants to ask the wizard's help to give him a brain. Loyal, kind, and thoughtful, this loving scarecrow makes fast friends.

HAIR COLOR: Yellow as straw

EYE COLOR: Blue as a sunny sky in Oz

LIKES:
- Dorothy
- Helping
- The Emerald City

DISLIKES:
- Scaring crows
- Feeling stupid
- Fire

The Tin Woodman

After a curse from the Wicked Witch of the West left him made completely of tin and stuck in the forest, the tin woodman craves a heart to remember what it was like to love his sweetheart. A tender soul, the tin woodman hates to hurt any creature, even by accident, and bravely puts his axe before danger many times to save his friends.

HAIR COLOR: Silver as Dorothy's slippers

EYE COLOR: Brown as rust

LIKES:
- Dorothy
- The Winkies
- Fresh oil

DISLIKES:
- The Wicked Witch of the West
- Rust
- Hurting living creatures

The Cowardly Lion

The cowardly lion wishes to be known as the King of the Beasts, but he is afraid of so many things that all he can do is roar at what scares him and hope he frightens it away. Desperate for courage, he follows along with the friends but often tries to face the danger alone in order to save them.

FUR COLOR: Golden yellow as tall grasses

EYE COLOR: Golden brown as glittering topaz

LIKES:
- Dorothy
- Gloomy forests
- Roaring

DISLIKES:
- The scarlet poppies
- Field mice
- Kahlidas

"You are welcome, most noble Sorceress, to the land of the Munchkins. We are so grateful to you for having killed the Wicked Witch of the East and for setting our people free from bondage."

Shocked, Dorothy finds herself in the Land of the East with the Munchkins, where her aunt and uncle's farmhouse appears to have landed directly on their evil ruler, the Wicked Witch of the East. While Dorothy is there, she meets the Good Witch of the North, who tells her to go to see the Wizard of Oz in the Emerald City in order to find her way back to Kansas.

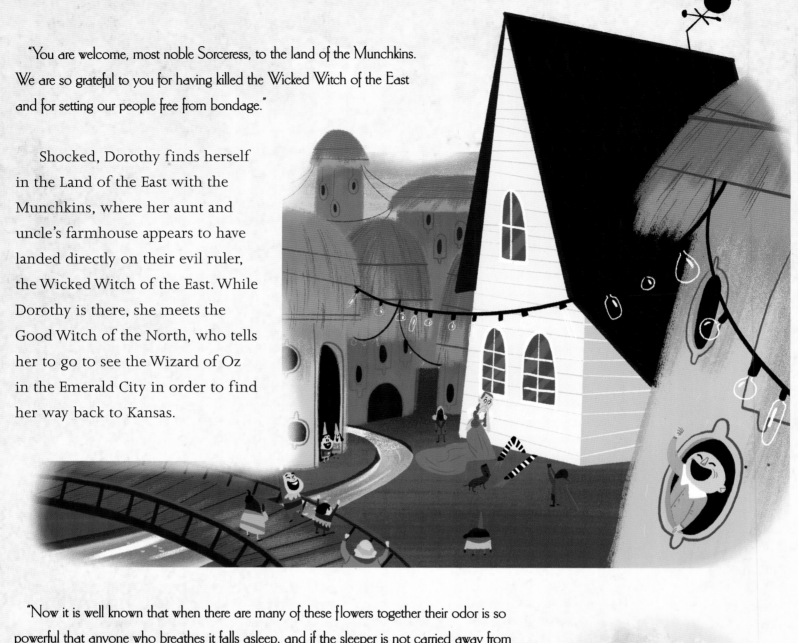

"Now it is well known that when there are many of these flowers together their odor is so powerful that anyone who breathes it falls asleep, and if the sleeper is not carried away from the scent of the flowers, he sleeps on and on forever. But Dorothy did not know this, nor could she get away from the bright red flowers that were everywhere about; so presently her eyes grew heavy and she felt she must sit down to rest and to sleep."

When Dorothy succumbs to the poisonous odor of the poppies, the scarecrow, tin woodman, and cowardly lion must find a way to rescue her. They rush to the other side of the field and come across a field mouse fleeing from a wildcat. Quickly slaying the wildcat, the tin woodman rescues the little creature, who introduces herself as the Queen of the Field Mice, and offers the service of her kingdom whenever they should need it.

"As it fell with a crash they looked that way, and the next moment all of them were filled with wonder. For they saw, standing in just the spot the screen had hidden, a little old man, with a bald head and a wrinkled face, who seemed to be as much surprised as they were. The tin woodman, raising his axe, rushed toward the little man and cried out, 'Who are you?'

'I am Oz, the Great and Terrible,' said the little man, in a trembling voice. 'But don't strike me—please don't—and I'll do anything you want me to.'"

After ridding the Land of the West of the Wicked Witch, Dorothy and her companions return to the Emerald City to get their reward from the wizard. But when Toto accidentally tears down the screen behind the wizard's throne, it is revealed that the many forms of the Wizard of Oz are merely costumes, and the wizard himself is but a man pretending to be both great and terrible. Worse still, he is unable to return Dorothy to her home, as he has no magic of his own.

"'Bless your dear heart,' she said, 'I am sure I can tell you of a way to get back to Kansas.' Then she added, 'But, if I do, you must give me the Golden Cap.'

'Willingly!' exclaimed Dorothy; 'indeed, it is of no use to me now, and when you have it you can command the Winged Monkeys three times.'

'And I think I shall need their service just those three times,' answered Glinda, smiling."

Glinda the Good Witch uses her magic to help Dorothy return to Kansas, and the kind witch uses the magical Flying Monkeys to return the scarecrow, the tin woodman, and the cowardly lion to the places they most wish to go. Freed by the Good Witch from the spell that enslaved them to the Wicked Witch of the West, the King of the Flying Monkeys and his people flee, finally free.

Kansas

Cowardly
Lion's
Forest

The Wicked Witch of the
West's Castle

The Emerald City

The River

Country of Quadlings

Bog's House

Thumbelina

Written in 1835 by Hans Christian Andersen, "Thumbelina" is a heartwarming story about a teeny, tiny girl who finds her place in the world. Thumbelina's story begins when a woman who desperately wants a child visits a witch who gives her a little barley seed to plant. The barley seed produces a lovely yellow and red flower, which blooms to reveal a little girl sitting inside, no taller than a thumb. The woman names her Thumbelina and gives her a little bed to sleep in and a room of her own. One night, a slimy toad sneaks into Thumbelina's little room and steals her away, crowing with delight over finding the perfect bride for her equally slimy son. Poor Thumbelina wakes up in the middle of a stream, stranded on a lily pad watching the two toads eagerly prepare a house of mud for her and her soon-to-be husband. Sobbing bitterly, she breaks down on the lily pad. The fish in the stream take pity on the lovely girl and chew the water lily's stem so that her pad moves with the flow of the stream and takes her far away. Through tall trees, thick grasses, and dark dens, Thumbelina is caught by so many creatures who want to marry her off. But when she saves a swallow from freezing to death, she makes a true friend who later helps her find her destiny as one of the flower folk—spirits of the blooms that live in warmth and light.

Thumbelina

Dainty and sweet, Thumbelina adores nature and loves being warmed by sunshine and listening to the birds sing. Although Thumbelina knows what she wants, her voice can get swept away by stronger personalities, and she tries to avoid disappointing anyone.

HAIR COLOR: Yellow as marigolds

EYE COLOR: Green as floating lily pads

LIKES:
- Sunshine
- Birdsong
- The swallow who rescues her

DISLIKES:
- The toads
- The mole
- Darkness

The Swallow ♫♪

    Carefree and happy, the swallow loves to chirp in the sunshine and soar through the air. He has a soft spot for Thumbelina, as she nurses him back to health when an injured wing leaves him unable to fly to warmer climates. Ever loyal, the swallow wants what is best for his friends.

FEATHER COLOR: Indigo with streaks of orange, like sunset becoming twilight

EYE COLOR: Black as beetle's wings

LIKES:
- Flying
- Singing
- Thumbelina

DISLIKES:
- The mole
- The winter
- Darkness

The Mole ♫

    Blind and solemn with a velvet black coat, the mole is a creature who has many admirers in the meadow. He is extremely wealthy and accustomed to people telling him anything he wants to hear in hopes that he'll share his possessions and his status. He detests the sunlight and knows nothing of flowers or trees, as he cannot see them.

FUR COLOR: Black as a deep, dark hole

EYE COLOR: Black as the darkest night

LIKES:
- Darkness
- Finery
- Dirt

DISLIKES:
- Sunlight
- Flowers
- Birds

The Toad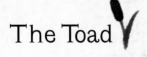

    The toad is a busybody, bold enough to kidnap Thumbelina from her home in order to set the poor girl up as a bride for her son. Aware that her actions are wrong, she anticipates Thumbelina wanting to escape and strands her on a distant lily pad until they are ready for her to join the toad's son.

SKIN COLOR: Dark green like thick reeds in a muddy marsh

EYE COLOR: Black as the bottom of the stream

LIKES:
- Meddling in her son's life
- Mud homes
- Arranged marriages

DISLIKES:
- Escaped hostages
- Dry land
- Not having control

"One night as she lay in her cradle, a horrible toad hopped in through the window—one of the panes was broken. This big, ugly, slimy toad jumped right down on the table where Thumbelina was asleep under the red rose petal."

Thumbelina is swept away from her slumber by a slimy toad and ushered into the toads' muddy marsh to become the wife of the toad's son. Seeing her crestfallen face, the fish of the nearby stream help her to escape. But soon Thumbelina is captured by a May bug, who sees her lovely face and wants to marry her. However, when the lady May bugs mock Thumbelina's two legs and lack of antennae, the bug changes his mind and flies off, stranding her in a tree.

"Poor Thumbelina stood at the door, just like a beggar child, and pled for a little bit of barley, because she hadn't had anything to eat for two days past."

After fleeing the tree and finding her way into a field, Thumbelina is freezing and near starving when she knocks on the field mouse's door. The field mouse takes her in and Thumbelina stays, telling stories and tidying up to earn her keep. But the field mouse plans to match her up with her neighbor, the mole, for he is very rich. Desperate not to offend her benefactor, Thumbelina goes along with the field mouse's plan.

"'Maybe it was he who sang so sweetly to me in the summertime,' she thought to herself. 'What pleasure he gave me, the dear, pretty bird.'"

When the mole discovers a dead bird in his tunnel, Thumbelina mourns its loss and, in her grief, attempts to warm it. She succeeds in nursing the bird back to health, as it was only the numbing cold that made it appear dead. The grateful swallow offers to help Thumbelina escape to warmer weather, far from the mole he knows she does not love.

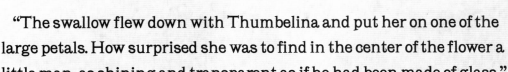

"The swallow flew down with Thumbelina and put her on one of the large petals. How surprised she was to find in the center of the flower a little man, as shining and transparent as if he had been made of glass."

When the swallow arrives in warmer weather with Thumbelina, he returns her to the flowers. She discovers that her people live here, and that she is a flower spirit, meant to live in the flowers with her people. The king is enamored with her delicate face and asks her to become his queen. The swallow flies back home, missing Thumbelina but happy that she is finally where she belongs.

WITCH'S HOME

THUMBELINA'S MOTHER'S HOME

TOAD MARSH

THUMBELINA

FIELD OF THE FLOWER FOLK

MOLE'S HOLE

FIELD MOUSE'S HOME

MAY BUG'S TREE

N
W   E
S

The Adventures of Pinocchio

Written in 1883 by Carlo Collodi, "The Adventures of Pinocchio" is a story about a puppet who comes to life and finds out what it means to be human. After Mastro Geppetto crafts a mischievous piece of talking wood into a marionette, he names it Pinocchio, and trouble ensues. The puppet is badly behaved and runs away, tricking the town policeman into thinking Geppetto, his father, is worthy of arrest. Returning home triumphant, Pinocchio is warned by the talking cricket to change his ways or regret it forever. Misery hits Pinocchio as he fails to remember the talking cricket's wise words, time and time again. His impish ways lead to him spending all of his schoolbook money on a scheme by two tricksters, Cat and Fox, nearly being robbed and killed by assassins, being thrown in jail, nearly drowned, turned into a donkey, and more! Pinocchio can't help but let his wickedness overtake his common sense, and continues to abandon school and family for the sake of his childish whims. All he needs to become a real boy is inside him, but can he learn his lesson and behave as a real boy should?

Pinocchio

Silly, mischievous, and easily distracted, Pinocchio has an earnest heart but an empty head. The marionette feels everything with his whole self: happiness, grief, anger, and love. Stubborn to a fault, he is desperate to do what is right—if only he can stop getting distracted by what is wrong.

HAIR COLOR: Black as burned firewood

EYE COLOR: Blue as painted porcelain

LIKES:
- Sugar
- Daydreaming
- The fairy

DISLIKES:
- School
- Studying
- Cat and Fox

Mastro Geppetto

Mastro Geppetto is a talented carpenter with an ugly temper. Enraged by Pinocchio's misbehavior but with a curious soft spot for his puppet son, Geppetto tries to discipline him so he learns the error of his ways. Mastro Geppetto manages to never hold a grudge, even when Pinocchio's antics lead to trouble for his loved ones.

HAIR COLOR: Gray as stormy skies

EYE COLOR: Brown as wood shavings

LIKES:
- Carpentry
- Pinocchio
- Dry land

DISLIKES:
- Disobedience
- Losing Pinocchio
- The Terrible Shark

The Talking Cricket

The talking cricket has lived in Geppetto's home for more than one hundred years. Unassuming with a gentle voice, he tries to warn Pinocchio of his folly throughout his journey, and though Pinocchio feels guilty for disregarding him, he does so often. In their first meeting, Pinocchio kills the talking cricket, but the cricket continues on as a ghost and a lesson.

SKIN COLOR: Green as spring grasses

EYE COLOR: Black as velvet

LIKES:
- Teaching
- The fairy
- Learning

DISLIKES:
- Bad little boys
- Hammers
- Being ignored

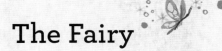

The Fairy

The fairy is a sweet, feminine spirit that guides Pinocchio on his journey. Despite his many mistakes, she is always willing to forgive him and has endless patience with his sense of mischief. Sometimes she appears as a little girl, sometimes as an older woman, but each time she offers Pinocchio guidance and love.

HAIR COLOR: Azure as calm ocean waves

EYE COLOR: Blue as dawn

LIKES:
- Pinocchio
- Disguises
- Teaching lessons

DISLIKES:
- Being ignored
- Runaway puppets
- Feeling hopeless

"'I'll explain,' said Fox. 'You must know that, just outside the City of Simple Simons, there is a blessed field called the Field of Wonders. In this field you dig a hole and in the hole you bury a gold piece. After covering up the hole with earth you water it well, sprinkle a bit of salt on it, and go to bed. During the night, the gold piece sprouts, grows, blossoms, and next morning you find a beautiful tree that is loaded with gold pieces.'"

After promising Mastro Geppetto that he will go to school, Pinocchio gets distracted by the Great Marionette Theater. He has great fun with the other marionettes and wins over the director's heart, earning him five gold coins. Before he can return home to give his father the unexpected windfall, he is diverted by cunning Cat and Fox, who convince him to follow them to the mysterious Field of Wonders.

"Lies, my boy, are known in a moment. There are two kinds of lies, lies with short legs and lies with long noses. Yours, just now, happen to have long noses."

When the fairy saves Pinocchio's life and cautions him to be a good boy, she explains that to live a happy life he must be truthful, well behaved, and productive. But just moments after he is saved from death, little Pinocchio cannot help but be mischievous. He lies about the location of his precious gold coins, and the lies are clear on his face as his nose grows with every fib. Pinocchio is ashamed by his long nose, as it confirms that he has been lying.

"This great land was entirely different from any other place in the world. Its population, large though it was, was composed wholly of boys. The oldest were about fourteen years of age, the youngest, eight. In the street, there was such a racket, such shouting, such blowing of trumpets, that it was deafening. Everywhere groups of boys were gathered together . . . The squares were filled with small wooden theaters, overflowing with boys from morning till night, and on the walls of the houses, written with charcoal, were words like these: 'HURRAH FOR THE LAND OF TOYS! DOWN WITH ARITHMETIC! NO MORE SCHOOL!'"

Despite promising the fairy that he would study hard and make something of himself, Pinocchio makes the mistake of trusting his friend Lamp-Wick on the eve of the day he was to become a real boy. Instead, they are taken to the Land of Toys, where they can evade school forever. But after five months of playing without working, the boys turn into donkeys! Unable to do anything, they are sold by the man who brought them there and realize their mistake at believing the land to be a utopia.

"'Oh, Father, dear Father! Have I found you at last? Now I shall never, never leave you again!'
'Are my eyes really telling me the truth?' answered the old man, rubbing his eyes. 'Are you really my own dear Pinocchio?'"

All hope seems lost as Pinocchio is swallowed and trapped inside the cavernous belly of the terrible shark. But as he searches for a way out, Pinocchio is finally reunited with his father, Mastro Geppetto, who was swallowed by the Terrible Shark nearly two years ago. Together they make it out of the shark, and Pinocchio cares for his ailing father endlessly, working hard to earn enough to make him comfortable and thinking little of himself. His journey taught him that these traits are worth more than gold and can have lasting impact on the path life lays out.

The Adventures of Pinocchio

The Fairy's White Cottage

City

The Inn of the Red Lobster

The Sea

School

Court House

Town

Talking Cricket's Home

Gepetto's Home

The Jungle Book

Written in 1894 by Rudyard Kipling, *The Jungle Book* is a tale of adventure, coming-of-age, and bravery. Saved from the tiger Shere Khan by a family of wolves, little Mowgli, the human boy, grows up in the heart of the jungle among the animals. Hunting, howling, and learning the language of the many creatures who live in the jungle from Baloo the bear, Mowgli is part of the pack. But unrest stirs in the jungle, and proud Shere Khan wants his revenge against Mowgli, who evaded capture many years ago. Shere Khan convinces the wolves that Mowgli does not belong with the pack, and they conspire to give the man-cub to Shere Khan, casting him out and into the jaws of the tiger. It soon becomes clear that Mowgli must find a balance between the two sides of himself: man and beast. With the help of his friend Bagheera the panther, and the love and support of his pack, Mowgli heads off in a wild tale of self-discovery and revenge against the tiger who hunts him. What will Mowgli decide: is he a man, or is he a wolf?

Mowgli

Wise beyond his years, Mowgli has the instincts of a wolf but the heart of a man. Most of his time is spent living and learning the Law of the Jungle, though he would always rather be hunting with his brothers than stuck learning from Old Baloo. Proud but mischievous, Mowgli still has the playful spirit of youth but meets any challenge to his home and family with courage and cunning.

HAIR COLOR: Black as the stripes of a tiger

EYE COLOR: Brown as the coils of Kaa's scaly skin

LIKES:
- Riding on Bagheera's back
- Running through the jungle with his brothers
- Revenge

DISLIKES:
- Baloo's boring lessons
- The crazy Bandar-log monkeys
- The fenced-in homes of men

Shere Khan

Born with a lame leg, lazy, and arrogant, tiger Shere Khan considers himself the King of the Jungle. But he is scorned by the rest of the animals for his pitiful hunting habits, as he brings the attention of villagers upon them all when he steals their fat cattle in the night. Shere Khan relies on sneaking and whispering to achieve his revenge, but his pride may be his downfall.

FUR COLOR: Orange as the sunset

EYE COLOR: Yellow-green as tall jungle grasses

LIKES:
- Eating slow cattle
- Being praised by Tabaqui the jackal
- Lording over the wolves

DISLIKES:
- Mowgli
- The wolves
- The Red Flower (fire)

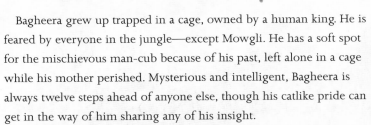

Bagheera

Bagheera grew up trapped in a cage, owned by a human king. He is feared by everyone in the jungle—except Mowgli. He has a soft spot for the mischievous man-cub because of his past, left alone in a cage while his mother perished. Mysterious and intelligent, Bagheera is always twelve steps ahead of anyone else, though his catlike pride can get in the way of him sharing any of his insight.

FUR COLOR: Black as a starless night

EYE COLOR: Gold as a sunrise

LIKES:
- The freedom to roam the jungle, feared by all
- Mowgli
- Hunting with cunning and grace

DISLIKES:
- Asking for help
- The Bandar-log monkeys
- Disrespect to his honor

Baloo

The gentle, bumbling, brown bear is Mowgli's teacher and friend. Although the man-cub often tries to escape his lessons, Baloo continues to teach him, knowing that his lessons are of grave importance to surviving the jungle. Although he can be rough with his paws, he is ultimately a pushover, caring about Mowgli with the tenderness of a father.

HAIR COLOR: Brown as the bark of the trees

EYE COLOR: Black as his shadow

LIKES:
- Mowgli
- Teaching wolf cubs
- Termites and ants

DISLIKES:
- Teaching wolf cubs
- The Bandar-log monkeys
- Shere Khan

"Then Shere Khan roared: 'Bah! What have we to do with this toothless fool? He is doomed to die! It is the man-cub who has lived too long. Free People, he was my meat from the first.

Give him to me. I am weary of this man-wolf folly. He has troubled the jungle for ten seasons. Give me the man-cub, or I will hunt here always, and not give you one bone.

He is a man, a man's child, and from the marrow of my bones I hate him!'

Then more than half the pack yelled: 'A man! A man! What has a man to do with us? Let him go to his own place.'"

After months of being fed with scraps and Shere Khan's lies, the young and foolish wolves of the pack are eager to kick Mowgli out of the jungle. It is in this scene that Shere Khan's motives are revealed: he wants Mowgli free from protection so he can make him a meal as he wanted to do so many years ago. Furious and hurt that his family is rejecting him, Mowgli goes, after threatening the wolves with the Red Flower of flame that only he can wield.

"Generations of monkeys had been scared into good behavior by the stories their elders told them of Kaa, the night thief, who could slip along the branches as quietly as moss grows and steal away the strongest monkey that ever lived; of old Kaa, who could make himself look so like a dead branch or a rotten stump that the wisest were deceived, till the branch caught them."

When the foolish Bandar-log monkeys kidnap Mowgli in order to gain the attention of the Jungle People, Baloo and Bagheera enlist the python Kaa in helping them rescue him. Sinister and fierce, Kaa is a force of destruction on the Lost City of the Bandar-log, and even Bagheera and Baloo almost get lost in his hypnotic movements and gaze.

"Then something began to hurt Mowgli inside him, as he had never been hurt in his life before, and he caught his breath and sobbed, and the tears ran down his face. 'What is it? What is it?' he said. 'I do not wish to leave the jungle, and I do not know what this is. Am I dying, Bagheera?'

'No, Little Brother. That is only tears such as men use,' said Bagheera. 'Now I know thou art a man, and a man's cub no longer. The jungle is shut indeed to thee henceforward. Let them fall, Mowgli. They are only tears.'"

When his family drives him out to join the world of men, Mowgli can't help but mourn the loss of his old life. As Bagheera points out to him, the human emotion of sadness and the display of tears only confirm that Mowgli belongs with mankind, not in the jungle. His sadness over leaving the jungle is a human trait, not an animal one.

"He put his hands to his mouth and shouted down the ravine—it was almost like shouting down a tunnel—and the echoes jumped from rock to rock. After a long time there came back the drawling, sleepy snarl of a full-fed tiger just wakened.

'Who calls?' said Shere Khan, and a splendid peacock fluttered up out of the ravine screeching.

'I, Mowgli. Cattle thief, it is time to come to the Council Rock!'"

Mowgli knows that Shere Khan will not rest until he is dead, so he forms a plan to rid the world of the devious tiger once and for all. Trapping the lazy beast in a ravine, he unleashes herds of buffalo with the help of his wolf brothers, and his enemy is trampled. Their old war is finished as the fierce tiger fades.

THE Jungle BOOK

MOWGLI'S
HOME CAVE

THE
SEEONEE
HILLS

COUNCIL
ROCK

BALOO'S
resting
place

BAGHEERA'S
HUNTING GROUND

KAA'S
HUNTING
GROUND

SHERE KHAN'S
HUNTING GROUND

ELEPHANTS' STOMPING GROUND

KHANIWARA Market

WAINGUNGA RIVER

THE VILLAGE of MEN

the RED flower

N

W

E

S

THE LOST CITY of the BANDAR-LOG

Little Red Riding Hood

The earliest print version of "Little Red Riding Hood" was written by Charles Perrault in the seventeenth century, but the story has been told in many variations dating back to the tenth century. The tale of Little Red Riding Hood remains a classic because of its simple message: always listen to your mother. When Little Red goes to deliver treats to her ill grandmother, she is waylaid by a sneaky wolf with dinner on his mind. Naïve to the wolf's motives, Little Red Riding Hood lets him trick her off of the forest path despite her mother's warnings. Donning disguises and lying smoothly, the wolf manages to sneak his way into Little Red's journey. Poor Little Red doesn't realize his motives until she and her grandmother both end up in the belly of the beast (literally!).

Little Red Riding Hood

Naïve, but earnest, Little Red Riding Hood always tries to do the right thing, but she can get easily distracted. Although she has a good heart, sometimes it doesn't lead her in the right direction. She loves her family and doesn't want them eaten by wolves.

HAIR COLOR: Pale yellow, like sunbeams winking through the trees

EYE COLOR: Blue as wildflower petals

LIKES:
- Wildflowers
- Birdsong
- Ignoring her mother's advice

DISLIKES:
- Hungry wolves
- Walking to school
- Blue, green, or yellow hoods

Big, Bad Wolf

Clever and sly, the Big, Bad Wolf is always hungry and on the hunt. When he sees Little Red Riding Hood innocently skipping through the forest, he knows he's found his meal ticket. Preferring to use his wits over his brute strength, he knows that patience and cunning will help him achieve his goal.

FUR COLOR: Gray as smoke

EYE COLOR: Yellow as dead grass

LIKES:
- Tasty grandmothers
- Scrumptious little girls
- Napping after a good meal

DISLIKES:
- Nosy huntsmen
- Being woken up
- Skipping meals

Grandmother

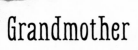

Little Red Riding Hood's grandmother eagerly looks forward to her granddaughter's visits, and the two lighten each other's spirits. It was Little Red Riding Hood's grandmother who first made the little one the red hood made of velvet, which became her namesake. Frail but loving, Little Red Riding Hood's grandmother would do anything for her granddaughter.

HAIR COLOR: Gray as a foggy day

EYE COLOR: Blue as a lake in summer

LIKES:
- Little Red Riding Hood
- Resting
- Flowers

DISLIKES:
- Hungry wolves
- Surprises
- Tight spaces

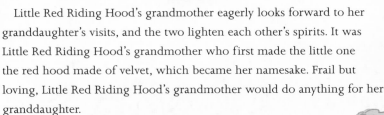

Huntsman

Familiar with the woods and brave enough to wade into the fray whenever he senses danger, the huntsman is an everyday hero. He has a strong sense of justice, and is always happy to help damsel(s) in distress if they ever find themselves being eaten, especially by his sinister nemesis, the Big, Bad Wolf.

HAIR COLOR: Brown as the trunk of an oak

EYE COLOR: Green as a new sapling

LIKES:
- Walks in the woods
- Saving the day
- Hunting

DISLIKES:
- The Big, Bad Wolf
- Missing shots
- Tricks

"'Come Little Red Riding Hood. Here is a piece of cake and a bottle of wine. Take them to your grandmother. She is sick and weak, and they will do her well. Mind your manners and give her my greetings. Behave yourself on the way, and do not leave the path . . .'"

Little Red Riding Hood's mother gives her very specific advice when she sends her to her grandmother's house, making sure to warn her not to stray from the path. Despite the best of Little Red's intentions, she can't seem resist the tempting distractions of the beautiful day.

"And she ran off the path into the woods looking for flowers. Each time she picked one, she thought that she could see an even more beautiful one a little way off, and she ran after it, going farther and farther into the woods. But the wolf ran straight to the grandmother's house and knocked on the door."

The wolf distracts Little Red Riding Hood by encouraging her to enjoy the beauty of the forest around her instead of trudging to her grandmother's house with single-minded determination. But as she searches for a bouquet for her ailing grandmother, the wolf sneaks off, up to mischief.

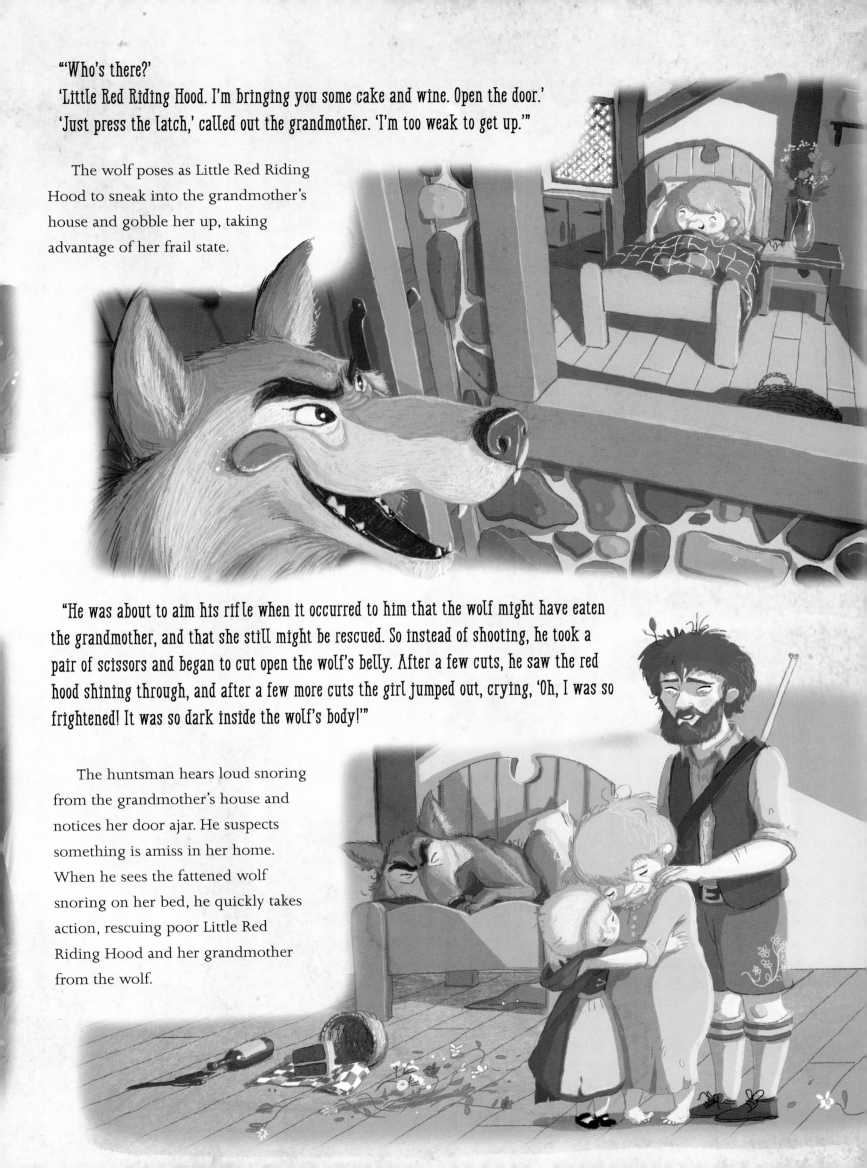

"'Who's there?'
'Little Red Riding Hood. I'm bringing you some cake and wine. Open the door.'
'Just press the latch,' called out the grandmother. 'I'm too weak to get up.'"

The wolf poses as Little Red Riding Hood to sneak into the grandmother's house and gobble her up, taking advantage of her frail state.

"He was about to aim his rifle when it occurred to him that the wolf might have eaten the grandmother, and that she still might be rescued. So instead of shooting, he took a pair of scissors and began to cut open the wolf's belly. After a few cuts, he saw the red hood shining through, and after a few more cuts the girl jumped out, crying, 'Oh, I was so frightened! It was so dark inside the wolf's body!'"

The huntsman hears loud snoring from the grandmother's house and notices her door ajar. He suspects something is amiss in her home. When he sees the fattened wolf snoring on her bed, he quickly takes action, rescuing poor Little Red Riding Hood and her grandmother from the wolf.

Grandmother's House

The Woods

THE E ND.

ILLUSTRATORS

Alice's Adventures in Wonderland: Khoa Le

"Jack and The Beanstalk": Anita Barghigiani

"The Little Mermaid": Morgan Huff

"Hansel and Gretel": Katie Melrose

"Little Snow White": Fabiana Attanasio

Peter Pan: Kelly Breemer

"Aladdin and the Wonderful Lamp": Mirelle Ortega

The Wonderful Wizard of Oz: James Sanchez

"Thumbelina": Carine Hinder

"The Adventures of Pinocchio": Benedetta Capriotti

The Jungle Book: Louise Pigott

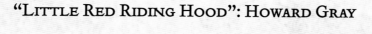

"Little Red Riding Hood": Howard Gray

Silver Dolphin Books
An imprint of Printers Row Publishing Group
A division of Readerlink Distribution Services, LLC
10350 Barnes Canyon Road, Suite 100, San Diego, CA 92121
www.silverdolphinbooks.com

Written by Courtney Acampora and Maggie Fischer
Designed by Mariel Lopez-Cotero
Hand lettering by Kelly Breemer

ISBN: 978-1-68412-623-1
Manufactured, printed, and assembled in Heshan, China.
First printing, February 2019. HH/02/19
23 22 21 20 19 1 2 3 4 5

Andersen, Hans Christian. "The Little Mermaid" in *Hans Christian Andersen Tales*. San Diego: Canterbury Classics, 2014.

Andersen, Hans Christian. "Thumbelina" in *Hans Christian Andersen Tales*. San Diego: Canterbury Classics, 2014.

Barrie, J. M. *Peter Pan*. San Diego: Canterbury Classics, 2017.

Baum, Frank L. *The Wonderful Wizard of Oz*. San Diego: Canterbury Classics, 2013.

Carroll, Lewis. *Alice's Adventures in Wonderland and Through the Looking-Glass*. San Diego: Canterbury Classics, 2016.

Collodi, Carlo. Translated by Carol Della Chiesa. *The Adventures of Pinocchio*. Scotts Valley: CreateSpace Independent Publishing Platform, 2014.

Grimm, Jacob and Wilhelm Grimm. "Hansel and Gretel" in *The Brothers Grimm 101 Fairy Tales*. San Diego: Canterbury Classics, 2012.

Grimm, Jacob and Wilhelm Grimm. "Little Red Cap" in *The Brothers Grimm 101 Fairy Tales*. San Diego: Canterbury Classics, 2012.

Grimm, Jacob and Wilhelm Grimm. "Little Snow White" in *The Brothers Grimm 101 Fairy Tales*. San Diego: Canterbury Classics, 2012.

Jacobs, Joseph. "Jack and the Beanstalk" in *English Fairy Tales*. London: David Nutt, 1890.

Kipling, Rudyard. *The Jungle Book*. San Diego: Canterbury Classics, 2014.

Unknown. Translated by Sir Richard F. Burton. "Aladdin and the Wonderful Lamp" in *Arabian Nights*. San Diego: Canterbury Classics, 2011.